MW00941078

#2

STEEL EYES

by Jonny Zucker

illustrated by
Paul Savage

Librarian Reviewer
Joanne Bongaarts
Educational Consultant
MS in Library Media Education, Minnesota State University, Mankato, MN
Teacher and Media Specialist with Edina Public Schools, MN, 1993–2000

Reading Consultant
Elizabeth Stedem
Educator/Consultant, Colorado Springs, CO
MA in Elementary Education, University of Denver, CO

 **STONE ARCH BOOKS**
Minneapolis   San Diego

First published in the United States in 2006
by Stone Arch Books,
151 Good Counsel Drive, P.O. Box 669,
Mankato, Minnesota 56002.
www.stonearchbooks.com

Originally published in Great Britain in 2005
by Badger Publishing Ltd.

Original work copyright © 2005 Badger Publishing Ltd
Text copyright © 2005 Jonny Zucker

Library of Congress Cataloging-in-Publication Data
Zucker, Jonny.
    Steel Eyes / by Jonny Zucker; illustrated by Paul Savage.
    p. cm. — Keystone Books.
    Summary: Even before he knows the truth, Gary is determined to
protect Emma, the new girl in school. Gail and Tanya will stop at nothing
to learn why Emma always wears sunglasses.
    ISBN-13: 978-1-59889-019-8 (hardcover)
    ISBN-10: 1-59889-019-0 (hardcover)
    ISBN-13: 978-1-59889-190-4 (paperback)
    ISBN-10: 1-59889-190-1 (paperback)
    [1. Sunglasses—Fiction. 2. Bullies—Fiction. 3. Schools—Fiction.
4. Horror stories—Fiction.] I. Savage, Paul, 1971– ill. II. Title.
PZ7.Z77925Ste 2006
[Fic]—dc22   2005026566

1 2 3 4 5 6 11 10 09 08 07 06

Printed in the United States of America

TABLE OF CONTENTS

Chapter 1

NEW GIRL

On Monday morning, a new girl arrived at Gary's school. She was wearing blue jeans, black boots, and a heavy jacket. She was also wearing sunglasses, even though it was a cloudy December day.

"Hi, I'm Emma Stone," she said, walking up to Gary.

"Gary Roper," he replied.

"Where can I get something to eat around here?" she asked.

"There's a vending machine near the music rooms," Gary replied.

They walked only a few steps when someone yelled, "Hey!"

Emma felt a tap on her shoulder. She and Gary turned around.

It was Tanya Swan. She was standing with Gail Jones. Tanya and Gail were the leaders of a gang called The Scars.

"What's with the sunglasses?"
Gail asked.

"Get rid of them!" Tanya ordered.
"Or do you think they make you
look cool?"

"And you are?" asked Emma.

"Don't talk back to me," scowled
Tanya. "Now, I thought I told you to
take those glasses off."

"If I took them off, you'd regret it,"
said Emma. "So I'd be careful what you
ask for."

Tanya stood with her mouth open.
It was a while before she spoke again.

"W- w- well, you'll be told to take them off," Tanya said. "No one's allowed to wear sunglasses in school."

And with that, Tanya and Gail stormed off.

Emma turned back to Gary. "Now, where's that vending machine?" she asked.

WHAT'S THE STORY?

Over the next couple of days, Gary hung out with Emma. They had fun together. They were both into art and music. Gary played guitar, and Emma played bass.

Gary soon found out that Tanya was wrong about Emma's sunglasses. Teachers didn't ask Emma to take them off.

In fact, they all seemed eager for her to keep them on.

Gary didn't ask Emma about the sunglasses, but he did wonder about them. If she was nearsighted or farsighted, why didn't she just wear normal glasses? Maybe one of her eyes was bigger than the other. Or she could be covering up a scar.

Gary was walking across the schoolyard Thursday morning when his path was blocked by Tanya, Gail, and other members of their gang.

"Let's hear it," said Tanya. "What's the story?"

"The story?" he asked.

"Yeah, the story about why your girlfriend is allowed to wear sunglasses in school," said Tanya. "I told her not to wear them anymore."

"She's not my girlfriend,"
Gary replied.

"Whatever!" exclaimed Gail. "Just
tell us what's going on."

Gary shrugged his shoulders.
"Don't know."

"Do you think we believe that?"
sneered Tanya.

Gary brushed the girls out of his way.

"It's the truth," he said. "I don't know why she wears them."

"Fine!" shouted Tanya. "We'll just find out for ourselves."

Chapter 3

WHISPERED CONVERSATION

On Friday afternoon, Gary was about to get something from his homeroom when he heard two people talking quietly inside.

It was Mr. Dalton and Mr. Reese.

"How's that Stone girl doing?" Mr. Reese asked.

"So far it's working out," Mr. Dalton replied. "Miss Harmon says Emma wears a headband during Phy. Ed. to keep her sunglasses from falling off."

"What about Swan and Jones? Are those girls harassing her?"

"They're all talk," said Mr. Dalton. "They seem to be leaving her alone."

"It's weird, though, isn't it?" said Mr. Reese. "I mean, that medical report you showed me was pretty strange."

They lowered their voices to a whisper. Gary couldn't hear them anymore, so he pushed the door open. They looked embarrassed as Gary walked in. He could see them thinking, 'Did Gary Roper hear what we were talking about?'

"Everything okay, Gary?" Mr. Dalton asked.

Gary picked up the pen he had left in the room earlier.

"Everything's fine," he replied, heading back toward the door.

But everything wasn't fine. He was beginning to feel very uneasy.

Chapter 4

A WARNING

When school was over that afternoon, Gary went to find Emma. His head was spinning. Should he tell her that the teachers were talking about her?

He walked into one of the art studios. Emma was sitting alone with her back to the door. Gary saw that her sunglasses were on the table next to her.

She was holding a small tube and putting drops into her eyes.

Gary sighed with relief. That must be it. She just had some sort of eye infection, and her eyes needed to be covered all of the time.

"Emma," he called out, walking past the drawing tables.

"Don't come any closer!" shouted Emma.

Gary froze in his tracks.

Emma quickly set the tube down and put her sunglasses back on. Seconds later, she turned around. The glasses covered her eyes.

"I- just- I," Gary didn't know where to start.

"It's okay, Gary," Emma said softly. "I think it's time I told you the truth."

Chapter 5

TIME FOR TROUBLE

In school the next week, Gary and Emma spent a lot of time together. They were talking about forming a band and were thinking about the kids they would ask to join.

Emma's story about her sunglasses was incredible, but Gary knew she was telling the truth.

During lunch break on Friday, Gary was putting his guitar case away when he noticed Tanya near the bike racks. She was talking on her cell phone. He heard her mention Emma's name. He moved closer and crouched down in front of a mountain bike.

"I heard her telling someone she's going to the lake after school," Tanya was saying, "to work on some of her stupid drawings."

Gary frowned. He had been to the lake last weekend to work on some sketches with Emma.

Tanya paused a second and then laughed. "Nice idea. Let's go after school and teach her a lesson."

Chapter 6

THE SHOWDOWN

Gary was nervous all afternoon. He didn't have any classes with Emma, and he didn't see her anywhere. After school, he hurried out of his last class to warn Emma about Gail and Tanya. She was nowhere to be seen. Emma must already be at the lake, Gary thought.

He checked his watch. He needed to get to the lake — fast.

Gary left the schoolyard and then turned right at the end of the street. He raced through the park gate and ran down the path to the lake.

The lake came into view. He spotted Emma on the other side, sitting on a bench with her art supplies. Then he saw Tanya and Gail.

"Emma!" he shouted.

She was too far away to hear him. He sprinted down the path. As he approached, he saw Tanya and Gail leaning over Emma.

"We're not asking for much," Tanya was saying. "We just don't like secrets. All we want to know is why you never take those sunglasses off. Tell us, and we'll leave you alone."

"You wouldn't understand," Emma replied.

"Try us," said Tanya.

"Back off!" shouted Gary.

The three girls turned around to face him.

"Oh look! It's Superman coming to save his poor girlfriend," laughed Gail.

"I mean it," said Gary.

"Go away, Gary. This has nothing to do with you," spat Tanya.

The girls turned back to Emma.

"Either you tell us," said Tanya, "or we'll find out for ourselves."

Chapter 7

STEEL EYES

Emma stood up. "Don't even think about it," she replied firmly.

In a split second, Tanya reached over and pulled the sunglasses from Emma's face.

They fell to the ground.

"You shouldn't have done that!" Emma shouted.

She quickly reached down to grab
the glasses, turning away from them.

"Don't look into her eyes!"
yelled Gary.

Tanya and Gail ignored him. Tanya
grabbed Emma's hair and pulled Emma's
head around to face her and Gail.

Tanya and Gail looked straight into Emma's eyes. They found themselves staring at two circles of smooth steel, each with a tiny hole in the middle.

"I told you to look away!" Gary screamed.

It was too late!

Tanya and Gail felt shooting pains in their hands and feet. The pains quickly spread. The girls looked down and watched in horror as every part of their bodies began to change.

Tanya and Gail tried to scream, but no sound came out of their mouths.

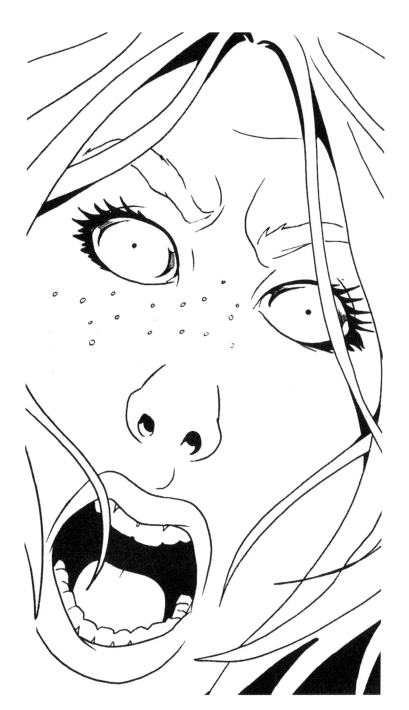

31

The last thing Tanya and Gail saw was Emma running down the path with Gary close behind her.

* * *

Later that afternoon, several kids from school walked down to the lake and saw two life-size statues.

They all agreed on one thing — the statues looked just like Tanya Swan and Gail Jones.

ABOUT THE AUTHOR

Even as a child, Jonny Zucker wanted to be a writer. Today, he has written over 30 books. He has also spent time working as a teacher, song writer, and stand-up comedian. Jonny lives in north London with his wife and two children.

ABOUT THE ILLUSTRATOR

Paul Savage works in a design studio, drawing pictures for advertising. He says illustrating books is "the best job." He's always been interested in illustrating books, and he loves reading. Paul also enjoys playing sports and running.

He lives in England with his wife and daughter, Amelia.

GLOSSARY

farsighted (FAR-site-uhd)—able to see faraway objects better than closer ones

infection (in-FEK-shuhn)—an illness caused by germs

nearsighted (NEER-sye-tid)—able to see nearby objects better than faraway ones

regret (ri-GRET)—to be sad or sorry about something

scowl (SKOWL)—to make an angry frown

sketch (SKECH)—a quick, rough drawing

sneer (SNEER)—to smile in a hateful, mocking way

sprint (SPRINT)—to run fast for a short distance

DISCUSSION QUESTIONS

1. Why are Tanya and Gail so curious about Emma? If you met Emma, would you be just as curious? Why or why not?

2. Gary doesn't ask Emma why she always wears sunglasses. Why does he wait until Emma tells him?

3. How does Emma feel about her power to turn people into statues? Explain your answer.

WRITING PROMPTS

1. Emma warns Tanya and Gail that something bad will happen if they take off her sunglasses, but they don't listen to her warnings. Write about a time you didn't listen to someone's warnings. What happened?

2. What if Emma was your sister, and you had a strange power, too. What would you be able to do? Describe how you would use your ability.

3. Imagine you are Gary. Write about what you would do after seeing Tanya and Gail turned into statues. Would you stay friends with Emma or be afraid of her ability?

ALSO BY JONNY ZUCKER

Basketball War

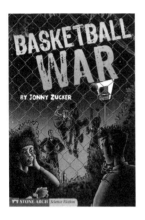

Jim and Ali are determined to beat the Langham Jets in the upcoming basketball championship. But the boys learn that there's something strange about their rival's new coach.

Skateboard Power

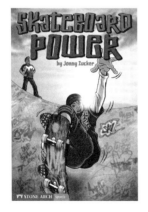

The skateboarding competition is just two weeks away, and Nick knows he's got a great shot at winning. But then the meanest kid in school tells Nick to stay out of the competition or else.

OTHER BOOKS IN THIS SET

Killer Sharks
by Stan Cullimore

The Brown family is relaxing on their speedboat when, suddenly, deadly sharks surround them — but these are no ordinary sharks. Who sent the killer sharks? And will the Browns get out alive?

Terror World
by Tony Norman

Jimmy and Seb love playing the games at Terror World arcade. When the owner offers them a free trial of a new game, they enter the real "Terror World." Chased by razor cats, it seems they have no escape.

INTERNET SITES

Do you want to know more about subjects related to this book? Or are you interested in learning about other topics? Then check out FactHound, a fun, easy way to find Internet sites.

Our investigative staff has already sniffed out great sites for you!

Here's how to use FactHound:

1. Visit *www.facthound.com*

2. Select your grade level.

3. To learn more about subjects related to this book, type in the book's ISBN number: **1598890190**.

4. Click the **Fetch It** button.

FactHound will fetch the best Internet sites for you!